RUSKIN BOND

GREAT STORIES
FOR CHILDREN
Volume 2

MOONSTONE

Published in Moonstone
by Rupa Publications India Pvt. Ltd 2023
7/16, Ansari Road, Daryaganj
New Delhi 110002

Sales centres:
Prayagraj Bengaluru Chennai
Hyderabad Jaipur Kathmandu
Kolkata Mumbai

P-ISBN: 978-93-5702-360-3
E-ISBN: 978-93-5702-356-6

First impression 2023

10 9 8 7 6 5 4 3 2 1

The moral right of the author has been asserted.

Printed in India

A Traveller's Tale

Gopalpur-on-sea!

A name to conjure with … and as a boy I'd heard it mentioned, by my father and others, and described as a quaint little seaside resort with a small port on the Orissa coast. The years passed, and I went from boyhood to manhood and eventually old age (is seventy-six old age? I wouldn't know) and still it was a place I'd only heard about and dreamt about but never visited.

Until last month, when I was a guest of KiiT International School in Bhubaneswar, and someone asked me where I'd like to go, and I said, 'Is Gopalpur very far?'

And off I went, along a palm-fringed highway, through busy little market-towns with names Rhamba and Humma, past the enormous Chilika lake which opens into the sea through paddy fields and keora plantations, and finally on to Gopalpur's beach road, with the sun glinting like gold on the great waves of the ocean, and the fishermen counting their catch, and the children sprinting into the sea, tumbling about in the shallows.

But the seafront wore a neglected look. The hotels were empty, the cafés deserted. A cheeky crow greeted me with a disconsolate caw from its perch on a weathered old wall. Some of the buildings were recent, but around us there were also the shells of older buildings that had fallen into ruin. And no one was going to preserve these relics of a colonial past. A small house called 'Brighton Villa' still survived.

But away from the seafront a tree-lined road took us past some well-maintained bungalows, a school, an old cemetery, and finally a PWD rest house where we were to spend the night.

It was growing dark when we arrived, and in the twilight, I could just make out the shapes of the trees that surrounded the old bungalow – a hoary old banyan, a jack-fruit and several mango trees. The light from the bungalow's veranda fell on some oleander bushes. A hawk moth landed on my shirt-front and appeared reluctant to leave. I took it between my fingers and deposited it on the oleander bush.

It was almost midnight when I went to bed. The rest-house staff – the caretaker and the gardener – went to some trouble to arrange a meal, but it was a long time coming.

The gardener told me the house had once

been the residence of an Englishman who had left the country at the time of Independence, some sixty years or more ago. Some changes had been carried out, but the basic structure remained – high-ceilinged rooms with skylights, a long veranda and enormous bathrooms. The bathroom was so large you could have held a party in it. But there was just one potty and a basin. You could sit on the potty and meditate, fixating your thoughts (or absence of thought) on the distant basin.

I closed all doors and windows, switched off all lights (I find it impossible to sleep with a light on), and went to bed.

It was a comfortable bed, and I soon fell asleep, only to be awakened by a light tapping on the window near my bed.

Probably a branch of the oleander bush, I thought, and fell asleep again. But there was more tapping, louder this time, and then I was fully awake.

I sat up in bed and drew aside the curtains.

There was a face at the window.

In the half-light from the veranda I could not make out the features, but it was definitely a human face.

Obviously someone wanted to come in, the caretaker perhaps, or the chowkidar. But then, why not knock on the door? Perhaps he had. The door was at the other end of the room, and I may not have heard the knocking.

I am not in the habit of opening my doors to strangers in the night, but somehow I did not feel threatened or uneasy, so I got up, unlatched the door, and opened it for my midnight visitor.

Standing on the threshold was an imposing figure.

A tall dark man, turbaned, and dressed all in white. He wore some sort of uniform – the kind worn by those immaculate doormen at five-star hotels; but a rare sight in Gopalpur-on-sea.

'What is it you want?' I asked. 'Are you staying here?'

He did not reply but looked past me, possibly through me, and then walked silently into the room. I stood there, bewildered and awestruck, as he strode across to my bed, smoothed out the sheets and patted down my pillow. He then walked over to the next room and came back with a glass and a jug of water, which he placed on the bedside table. As if that were not enough, he picked up my day clothes, folded them neatly and placed them on a vacant chair. Then, just as unobtrusively and without so much

as a glance in my direction,
he left the room and walked
out into the night.

Early next morning, as the sun came up like thunder over the Bay of Bengal, I went down to the sea again, picking my way over the puddles of human excreta that decorated parts of the beach. Well, you can't have everything. The world might be more beautiful without the human presence; but then, who would appreciate it?

Back at the rest house for breakfast, I was reminded of my visitor of the previous night.

'Who was the tall gentleman who came to my room last night?' I asked. 'He looked like a butler. Smartly dressed, very dignified.'

The caretaker and the gardener exchanged meaningful glances.

You tell him,' said the caretaker to his companion.

'It must have been Hazoor Ali,' said the gardener, nodding. 'He was the orderly, the personal servant of Mr Robbins, the port commissioner – the Englishman who lived here.'

'But that was over sixty years ago,' I said. 'They must all be dead.'

'Yes, all are dead, sir. But sometimes the ghost of Hazoor Ali appears, especially if one of our guests reminds him of his old master. He was quite devoted to him, sir. In fact, he received this bungalow as a parting gift when Mr Robbins left the country. But unable to maintain it, he sold it to the government and returned to his home in Cuttack. He died many years ago, but revisits this place sometimes. Do not feel alarmed, sir. He means no harm. And he does not appear to everyone – you are the lucky one this year! I have but seen him twice. Once, when I took service here twenty years ago, and then, last year, the night before the cyclone. He came to warn us, I think. Went to every door and window and made sure they were secured.

Never said a word. Just vanished into the night.'

'And it's time for me to vanish by day,' I said, getting my things ready. I had to be in Bhubaneswar by late afternoon, to board the plane for Delhi. I was sorry it had been such a short stay. I would have liked to spend a few days in Gopalpur, wandering about its backwaters, old roads, mango groves, fishing villages, sandy inlets … Another time perhaps. In this life, if I am so lucky. Or the next, if I am luckier still.

At the airport in Bhubaneswar, the security asked me for my photo-identity. 'Driving licence, pan-card, passport? Anything with your picture on it will do, since you have an e-ticket,' he explained.

I do not have a driving licence and have never felt the need to carry my pan-card with me. Luckily, I always carry my passport on my travels. I looked for it in my little travel-bag and then in my suitcase, but couldn't find it. I was feeling awkward fumbling in all my pockets, when another senior officer came to my rescue. 'It's all right. Let him in. I know Mr Ruskin Bond,' he called out, and beckoned me inside.

I thanked him and hurried into the check-in area.

All the time in the flight, I was trying to recollect where I might have kept my passport. Possibly tucked away somewhere inside the suitcase, I thought. Now that my baggage was sealed at the airport,

I decided to look for it when I reached home.

A day later I was back in my home in the hills, tired after a long road journey from Delhi. I like travelling by road, there is so much to see, but the ever-increasing volume of traffic turns it into an obstacle race most of the time. To add to my woes, my passport was still missing. I looked for it everywhere – my suitcase, travel-bag, in all my pockets.

I gave up the search. Either I had dropped it somewhere, or I had left it at Gopalpur. I decided to ring up and check with the rest house staff the next day. It was a frosty night, bitingly cold, so I went to bed early, well covered with razai and blanket. Only two nights previously I had been sleeping under a fan!

It was a windy night, the windows were rattling; and the old tin roof was groaning, a loose sheet flapping about and making a frightful din. I slept only fitfully.

When the wind abated, I heard someone knocking on my front door.

'Who's there?' I called, but there was no answer.

The knocking continued, insistent, growing louder all the time.

'Who's there? *Kaun hai*?' I call again.

Only that knocking persisted.

Someone in distress, I thought. I'd better see who it is. I got up shivering, and walked barefoot to the front door. Opened it slowly, opened it wider, someone stepped out of the shadows.

Hazoor Ali salaamed, entered the room, and as in Gopalpur, he walked silently into the room. It was lying in disarray because of my frantic search for my passport. He arranged the room, removed my garments from my travel-bag, folded them and placed them neatly upon the cupboard shelves.

Then, he did a salaam again and waited at the door.

Strange, I thought. If he did the entire room, why did he not set the travel-bag in its right place? Why did he leave it lying on the floor? Possibly he didn't know where to keep it; he left the last bit of work for me. I picked up the bag to place it on the top shelf. And there, from its front pocket my passport fell out, onto the floor.

I turned to look at Hazoor Ali, but he had already walked out into the cold darkness.

When the Trees Walked

One morning while I was sitting beside Grandfather on the veranda steps, I noticed the tendril of a creeping vine trailing nearby. As we sat there in the soft sunshine of a north Indian winter, I saw the tendril moving slowly towards Grandfather. Twenty minutes later, it had crossed the step and was touching his feet

There is probably a scientific explanation for the plant's behaviour – something to do with light and warmth, perhaps – but I liked to think it moved across the steps simply because it wanted to be near Grandfather. One always felt like drawing close to him. Sometimes when I sat by myself beneath a tree, I would feel rather lonely but as soon as Grandfather joined me, the garden became a happy place. Grandfather had served many years in the Indian Forest Service and it was natural that he should know trees and like them. On his retirement, he built a bungalow on the outskirts of Dehradun, planting trees all around. Lime, mango, orange and guava, also eucalyptus, jacaranda, and Persian lilacs. In the fertile Doon Valley, plants and trees grew tall and strong.

There were other trees in the compound before the house was built, including an old peepul that had forced its way through the walls of an abandoned outhouse, knocking the bricks down with its vigorous growth. Peepul trees are great show offs. Even when there is no breeze, their broad-chested, slim-waisted leaves will spin like tops determined to attract your attention and invite you into the shade. Grandmother had wanted the peepul tree cut down but Grandfather had said, 'Let it be, we can always build another outhouse.

Grandmother didn't mind trees, but she preferred growing flowers and was constantly ordering catalogues and seeds. Grandfather helped her out with the gardening not because he was crazy about flower gardens but because he liked watching butterflies and 'there's only one way to attract butterflies,' he said, 'and that is to grow flowers for them.'

Grandfather wasn't content with growing trees in our compound. During the rains, he would walk into the jungle beyond the river-bed armed with cuttings and saplings which he would plant in the forest. 'But no one ever comes here!' I had protested, the first time we did this. 'Who's going to see them?'

'See, we're not planting them simply to improve the view,' replied Grandfather. 'We're planting them for the forest and for the animals and birds who live here and need more food and shelter.'

'Of course, men need trees too,' he added. 'To keep the desert away, to attract rain, to prevent the banks of rivers from being washed away, for fruits and flowers, leaves and seeds. Yes, for timber too. But men are cutting down trees without replacing them and if we don't plant a few trees ourselves, a time will come when the world will be one great desert.'

The thought of a world without trees became a sort of nightmare to me and I helped Grandfather in his tree-planting with greater enthusiasm. And while we went about our work, he taught me a poem by George Morris:

Woodman, spare that tree!

Touch not a single bough!

In youth it sheltered me,

And I'll protect it now.

'One day the trees will move again,' said Grandfather. 'They've been standing still for thousands of years but there was a time when they could walk about like people. Then along came an interfering busybody who cast a spell over them, rooting them to one place. But they're always trying to move. See how they reach out with their arms! And some of them, like the banyan tree with its travelling aerial roots, manage to get quite far. We found an island, a small rocky island in a dry river-bed. It was one of those river-beds so common in the foothills, which are completely dry in summer but flooded during the monsoon rains. A small mango was growing on the island. 'If a small tree can grow here,' said Grandfather, 'so can others.' As soon as the rains set in and while rivers could still be crossed, we set out with a number of tamarind, laburnum, and coral tree saplings and cuttings and spent the day planting them on the island.

The monsoon season was the time for rambling about. At every turn, there was something new to see. Out of the earth and rock and leafless boughs, the magic touch of the rains had brought life and greenness. You could see the broad-leaved vines growing. Plants sprang up in the most unlikely of places. A peepul would take root in the ceiling, a mango would sprout on the window-sill. We did not like to remove them but they had to go if the house was to be kept from falling down.

'If you want to live in a tree, that's all right by me,' said Grandmother crossly. 'But I like having a roof over my head and I'm not going to have

my roof brought down by the jungle.'

Then came the Second World War and I was sent away to a boarding school. During the holidays, I went to live with my father in Delhi. Meanwhile, my grandparents sold the house and went to England. Two or three years later, I too went to England and was away from India for several years. Some years later, I returned to Dehradun. After first visiting the old house – it hadn't changed much – I walked out of town towards the river-bed. It was February. As I looked across the dry water-course,

my eye was immediately caught by the spectacular red blooms of the coral blossom. In contrast with the dry river-bed, the island was a small green paradise. When I went up to the trees, I noticed that some squirrels were living in them and a koel. A crow pheasant, challenged me with a mellow '**who-are-you, who-are-you**'. (An older Ruskin Bond comes across his island that he and his grandfather had planted trees in, to see it teeming with green trees and birds of all kinds).

But the trees seemed to know me; they whispered among themselves and beckoned me nearer.

And looking around I noticed that other smaller trees, wild plants and grasses had sprung up under their protection. Yes, the trees we had planted long ago had multiplied. They were walking again. In one small corner of the world, Grandfather's dream had come true.

Pret in the House

It was Grandmother who decided that we must move to another house. And it was all because of a pret, a mischievous ghost, who had been making life intolerable for everyone.

In India, prets usually live in peepul trees, and that's where our Pret first had his abode – in the branches of an old peepul which had grown through the compound wall and had spread into the garden, on our side, and over the road, on the other side.

For many years, the Pret had lived there quite happily, without bothering anyone in the house. I suppose the traffic on the road had kept him fully occupied. Sometimes, when a tonga was passing, he would frighten the pony and, as a result, the little pony-cart would go reeling off the road. Occasionally he would get into the engine of a car or bus, which would soon afterwards have a breakdown. And he liked to knock the sola-topis off the heads of sahibs, who would curse and wonder how a breeze had sprung up so suddenly, only to die down again just as quickly. Although the Pret could make himself felt, and sometimes heard, he was invisible to the human eye.

At night, people avoided walking beneath the peepul tree. It was said that if you yawned beneath the tree, the Pret would jump down your throat and ruin your digestion. Grandmother's tailor, Jaspal, who never had anything ready on time, blamed the Pret for all his troubles. Once, when yawning, Jaspal had forgotten to snap his fingers in front of his mouth – always mandatory when yawning beneath peepul trees – and the Pret had got in without any difficulty. Since then, Jaspal had always been suffering from tummy upsets.

But it had left our family alone until, one day, the

peepul tree had been cut down.

It was nobody's fault except, of course, that Grandfather had given the Public Works Department permission to cut the tree which had been standing on our land. They wanted to widen the road, and the tree and a bit of wall were in the way; so both had to go. In any case, not even a ghost can prevail against the PWD. But hardly a day had passed when we discovered that the Pret, deprived of his tree, had decided to take up residence in the bungalow.

And since a good Pret must be bad in order to justify his existence, he was soon up to all sorts of mischief in the house.

He began by hiding Grandmother's spectacles whenever she took them off.

'I'm sure I put them down on the dressing-table,' she grumbled.

A little later they were found balanced precariously on the snout of a wild boar, whose stuffed and mounted head adorned the veranda wall. Being the only boy in the house, I was at first blamed for this prank; but a day or two later, when the spectacles disappeared again only to be discovered dangling from the wires of the parrot's cage, it was agreed that some other agency was at work.

Grandfather was the next to be troubled. He went into the garden one morning to find all his prized sweet-peas snipped off and lying on the ground.

Uncle Ken was the next to suffer. He was a heavy sleeper, and once he'd gone to bed, he hated being woken up. So when he came to the breakfast table looking bleary-eyed and miserable, we asked him if he was feeling all right.

'I couldn't sleep a wink last night,' he complained. 'Every time I was about to fall asleep, the bedclothes would be pulled off the bed. I had to get up at least a dozen times to pick them off the floor.' He stared balefully at me. 'Where were you sleeping last night, young man?'

I had an alibi. 'In Grandfather's room,' I said.

'That's right,' said Grandfather. 'And I'm a light sleeper. I'd have woken up if he'd been sleep-walking.'

'It's that ghost from the peepul tree,' said Grandmother.

'It has moved into the house. First my spectacles, then the sweet-peas, and now Ken's bedclothes! What will it be up to next? I wonder!'

We did not have to wonder for long. There followed a series of disasters. Vases fell off tables, pictures came down the walls. Parrot feathers turned up in the teapot while the parrot himself let out indignant squawks in the middle of the night. Uncle Ken found a crow's nest in his bed, and on tossing it out of the window was attacked by two crows.

When Aunt Minnie came to stay, things got worse.

The Pret seemed to take an immediate dislike to Aunt Minnie. She was a nervous, easily excitable person, just the right sort of prey for a spiteful ghost. Somehow her toothpaste got switched with a tube of Grandfather's shaving-cream, and when she appeared in the sitting-room, foaming at the mouth, we ran for our lives. Uncle Ken was shouting that she'd contracted rabies.

Two days later Aunt Minnie complained that she had been hit on the nose by a grapefruit, which, according to her, had of its own accord leapt from the pantry shelf and hurtled across the room straight at her. A bruised and swollen nose testified to the attack. Aunt Minnie swore that life had been more peaceful in Upper Burma.

'We'll have to leave this house,' declared Grandmother.

'If we stay here much longer, both Ken and Minnie will have nervous breakdowns.'

'I thought Aunt Minnie broke down long ago,' I said.

'None of your cheek!' snapped Aunt Minnie.

'Anyway, I agree about changing the house,' I said breezily. 'I can't even do my homework. The ink-bottle is always empty.'

'There was ink in the soup last night,' came from Grandfather.

And so, a few days and several disasters later, we began moving to a new house.

Two bullock-carts laden with furniture and heavy luggage were sent ahead. The roof of the old car was piled high with bags and kitchen utensils. Everyone squeezed into the car, and Grandfather took the driver's seat.

We were barely out of the gate when we heard a peculiar sound, as if someone was chuckling and talking to himself on the roof of the car.

'Is the parrot out there on the luggage-rack?' the query came from Grandfather.

'No, he's in the cage on one of the bullock-carts,' said Grandmother.

Grandfather stopped the car, got out, and took a look at the roof.

'Nothing up there,' he said, getting in again and starting the engine. 'I'm sure I heard the parrot talking.'

Grandfather had driven some way up the road when the chuckling started again, followed by a squeaky little voice.

We all heard it. It was the Pret talking to itself.

'Let's go, let's go!' it squeaked gleefully. 'A new house. I can't wait to see it. What fun we're going to have!'

The Tunnel

It was almost noon, and the jungle was very still, very silent. Heat waves shimmered along the railway embankment where it cut a path through the tall evergreen trees. The railway lines were two straight black serpents disappearing into the tunnel in the hillside.

Suraj stood near the cutting, waiting for the mid-day train. It wasn't a station, and he wasn't catching a train. He was waiting so that he could watch the steam-engine come roaring out of the tunnel.

He had cycled out of the town and taken the jungle path until he reached a small village. He had left the cycle there, and walked over a low, scrub-covered hill and down to the tunnel exit.

Now he looked up. He had heard, in the distance, the shrill whistle of the engine. He couldn't see anything, because the train was approaching from the other side of the hill; but presently a sound, like distant thunder, issued from the tunnel, and he knew the train was coming through.

A second or two later, the steam-engine shot out of the tunnel, snorting and puffing like some green, black and gold dragon, some beautiful monster out of Suraj's dreams. Showering sparks left and right, it roared a challenge to the jungle.

Instinctively, Suraj stepped back a few paces. And then the train had gone, leaving only a plume of smoke to drift lazily over tall shisham trees.

The jungle was still again. No one moved. Suraj turned from his contemplation of the drifting smoke and began walking along the embankment towards the tunnel.

The tunnel grew darker as he walked further into it. When he had gone about twenty yards, it became pitch black. Suraj had to turn and look back at the opening to reassure himself that there was still daylight outside. Ahead of him, the tunnel's other opening was just a small round circle of light.

The tunnel was still full of smoke from the train, but it would be several hours before another train came through. Till then, it belonged to the jungle again.

Suraj didn't stop, because there was nothing to do in the tunnel and nothing to see. He had simply wanted to walk through, so that he would know what the inside of a tunnel was really like.

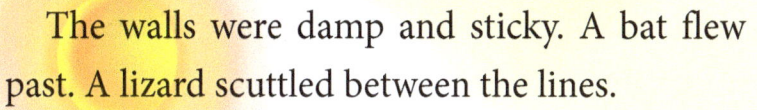

The walls were damp and sticky. A bat flew past. A lizard scuttled between the lines.

Coming straight from the darkness into the light, Suraj was dazzled by the sudden glare. He put a hand up to shade his eyes and looked up at the tree-covered hillside. He thought he saw something moving between the trees.

It was just a flash of orange and gold, and a long swishing tail. It was there between the trees for a second or two, and then it was gone.

About fifty feet from the entrance to the tunnel stood the watchman's hut. Marigolds grew in front of the hut, and at the back there was a small vegetable patch. It was the watchman's duty to inspect the tunnel and keep it clear of obstacles. Every day, before the train came through, he would walk the length of the tunnel. If all was well, he would return to his hut and take a nap.

If something was wrong, he would walk back up the line and wave a red flag and the engine-driver would slow down. At night, the watchman lit an oil lamp and made a similar inspection of the tunnel. Of course, he could not stop the train if there was a porcupine on the line. But if there was any danger to the train, he'd go back up the line and wave his lamp at the approaching engine. If all was well, he'd hang his lamp at the door of the hut and go to sleep.

He was just settling down on his cot for an afternoon nap when he saw the boy emerge from the tunnel. He waited until Suraj was only a few feet away and then said: 'Welcome, welcome, I don't often have visitors. Sit down for a while, and tell me why you were inspecting my tunnel.'

'Is it your tunnel?' asked Suraj.

'It is,' said the watchman. 'It is truly my tunnel, since no one else will have anything to do with it. I have only lent it to the government.'

Suraj sat down on the edge of the cot.

'I wanted to see the train come through,' he said. 'And then, when it had gone, I thought I'd walk through the tunnel.'

'And what did you find in it?'

'Nothing. It was very dark. But when I came out, I thought I saw an animal – up on the hill – but I'm not sure, it moved away very quickly.'

'It was a leopard you saw,' said the watchman. 'My leopard.'

'Do you own a leopard too?'

'I do.'

'And do you lend it to the government?'

'I do not.'

'Is it dangerous?'

'No, it's a leopard that minds its own business. It comes to this range for a few days every month.'

'Have you been here a long time?' asked Suraj.

'Many years. My name is Sunder Singh.'

'My name's Suraj.'

'There's one train during the day. And another at night. Have you seen the night mail come through the tunnel?'

'No. At what time does it come?'

'About nine o'clock, if it isn't late. You could come and sit here with me, if you like. And after it has gone, I'll take you home.'

'I shall ask my parents,' said Suraj. 'Will it be safe?'

'Of course. It's safer in the jungle than in the town. Nothing happens to me out here, but last month when I went into the town, I was almost run over by a bus.'

Sunder Singh yawned and stretched himself out on the cot. 'And now I'm going to take a nap, my friend. It is too hot to be up and about in the afternoon.'

'Everyone goes to sleep in the afternoon,' complained Suraj. 'My father lies down as soon as he's had his lunch.'

'Well, the animals also rest in the heat of the day. It is only the tribe of boys who cannot, or will not, rest.'

Sunder Singh placed a large banana-leaf over his face to keep away the flies, and was soon snoring gently. Suraj stood up, looking up and down the railway tracks. Then he began walking back to the village.

The following evening, towards dusk, as the flying foxes swooped silently out of the trees, Suraj made his way to the watchman's hut.

It had been a long hot day, but now the earth was cooling, and a light breeze was moving through the trees. It carried with it a scent of mango blossoms, the promise of rain.

Sunder Singh was waiting for Suraj. He had watered his small garden, and the flowers looked cool and fresh. A kettle was boiling on a small oil-stove.

'I'm making tea,' he said. 'There's nothing like a glass of hot tea while waiting for a train.'

They drank their tea, listening to the sharp notes of the tailorbird and the noisy chatter of the seven-sisters. As the brief twilight faded, most of the birds fell silent. Sunder Singh lit his oil-lamp and said it was time for him to inspect the tunnel. He moved off towards the tunnel, while Suraj sat on the cot, sipping his tea. In the dark, the trees seemed to move closer to him. And the night life of the forest was conveyed on the breeze – the sharp call of a barking-deer, the cry of a fox, the quaint tonk-tonk of a nightjar. There were some sounds that Suraj couldn't recognise – sounds that came from the trees, creakings and whisperings, as though the trees were coming alive, stretching their limbs in the dark, shifting a little, reflexing their fingers.

Sunder Singh stood inside the tunnel, trimming his lamp. The night sounds were familiar to him and he did not give them much thought; but something else – a padded footfall, a rustle of dry leaves – made him stand alert for a few seconds, peering into the darkness. Then, humming softly to himself, he returned to where Suraj was waiting. Another ten minutes remained for the night mail to arrive.

As Sunder Singh sat down on the cot beside Suraj, a new sound reached both of them quite distinctly – a rhythmic sawing sound, as if someone was cutting through the branch of a tree.

'What's that?' whispered Suraj.

'It's the leopard,' said Sunder Singh.

'I think it's in the tunnel.'

'The train will soon be here,' reminded Suraj.

'Yes, my friend. And if we don't drive the leopard out of the tunnel, it will be run over and killed. I can't let that happen.'

'But won't it attack us if we try to drive it out?' asked Suraj, beginning to share the watchman's concern.

'Not this leopard. It knows me well. We have seen each other many times. It has a weakness for goats and stray dogs, but it won't harm us. Even so, I'll take my axe with me. You stay here, Suraj.'

'No, I'm going with you. It'll be better than sitting here alone in the dark!'

'All right, but stay close behind me. And remember, there's nothing to fear.'

Raising his lamp high, Sunder Singh advanced into the tunnel, shouting at the top of his voice to try and scare away the animal. Suraj followed close behind, but he found he was unable to shout. His throat was quite dry.

They had gone just about twenty paces into the tunnel when the light from the lamp fell upon the leopard. It was crouching between the tracks, only fifteen feet away from them. It was not a very big leopard, but it looked lithe and sinewy. Baring its teeth and snarling, it went down on its belly, its tail twitching.

Suraj and Sunder Singh both shouted together. Their voices rang through the tunnel. And the leopard, uncertain as to how many terrifying humans were there in the tunnel with it, turned swiftly and disappeared into the darkness.

To ensure that it had gone, Sunder Singh and Suraj walked the length of the tunnel. When they returned to the entrance, the rails were beginning to hum. They knew the train was coming.

Suraj put his hand on the rails and felt its tremor. He heard the distant rumble of the train. And then the engine came round the bend, hissing at them, scattering sparks into the darkness, defying the jungle as it roared through the steep sides of the cutting. It charged straight at the tunnel, and into it, thundering past Suraj like the beautiful dragon of his dreams.

And when it had gone, the silence returned and the forest seemed to breathe, to live again. Only the rails still trembled with the passing of the train.

And they trembled to the passing of the same train, almost a week later, when Suraj and his father were both travelling in it.

Suraj's father was scribbling in a notebook, doing his accounts. Suraj sat at an open window staring out at the darkness. His father was going to Delhi on a business trip and had decided to take the boy along. ('I don't know where he gets to, most of the time,' he'd complained. 'I think it's time he learnt something about my business.')

The night mail rushed through the forest with its hundreds of passengers. Tiny flickering lights came and went, as they passed small villages on the fringe of the jungle.

Suraj heard the rumble as the train passed over a small bridge. It was too dark to see the hut near the cutting, but he knew they must be approaching the tunnel.

He strained his eyes looking out into the night; and then, just as the engine let out a shrill whistle, Suraj saw the lamp.

He couldn't see Sunder Singh, but he saw the lamp, and he knew that his friend was out there.

The train went into the tunnel and out again; it left the jungle behind and thundered across the endless plains; and Suraj stared out at the darkness, thinking of the lonely cutting in the forest, and the watchman with the lamp who would always remain a firefly for those travelling thousands, as he lit up the darkness for steam-engines and leopards.

www.ingramcontent.com/pod-product-compliance
Lightning Source LLC
Chambersburg PA
CBHW070043030726
47506CB00003B/843